FOR MADELEINE AND IAN
B. M.

&

FOR ALL THE HOMELESS CATS IN NEW YORK CITY
D. Z.

CALLAWAY

64 Bedford Street
New York, New York 10014

Printed in China by Palace Press International

FIRST EDITION

10 9 8 7 6 5 4 3 2 1

Library of Congress Cataloging-in-Publication Data available.

ISBN 0-935112-44-8

Visit Callaway at www.callaway.com

Antoinette White, Senior Editor   Jennifer Wagner, Designer

CRISPIN
THE TERRIBLE

WRITTEN BY BOB MORRIS

ILLUSTRATED BY DASHA ZIBOROVA

CALLAWAY

NEW YORK · 2000

My name is Crispin.

I'm a family cat. At least, that's what my family likes to think.

To them, family cat means stay-at-home cat. It means something to treat like a rag-doll, or ignore like a piece of furniture! I mean, just look at what I have to put up with!

My life is no bowl of tuna.

And I'm always so patient and good. But am I ever rewarded for it? Do I get any time off? Do they ever let me do what *I* want? No!

Things are going to change around here. Cats, after all, are supposed to have nine lives, and I haven't even had my first. So, good-bye Crispin the Good. Hello, Crispin the Terrible!

I could be very naughty if I wanted. I could unarrange the flowers
and delete stuff on the computer. And although I never used to meow,
I will now. Especially during quiet time.

Maybe I'll just run away — to the other side of the world!

I'll be *Crispin the Explorer!*

I could go to the airport and switch
places with a Japanese cat.

Imagine how great life would be in a Japanese fishing village.

Maybe I'll meet a Japanese kitty . . .

I could eat fish until the cows come home.

I'll be *Crispin the Samurai!*

Of course, I don't speak Japanese, so there might be
some misunderstanding. Then I'd really be in trouble.

I'd get sent home for sure. Probably in a box.
That would be so uncomfortable.

Okay. Forget Japan. Maybe I could go somewhere
that isn't quite so far away.

I could fly a model airplane to the country.

I would climb up a tree out of everybody's reach. I could stay up there forever.

Ah, the great outdoors! I'll be Crispin the Country Cat!

But, um, what would happen after dark? It gets rather chilly outside, right? Not to mention dangerous. I'm no fraidy cat, but there might be wild animals out there, like owls and bats and mosquitos. Maybe I'd be better off a little closer to home.

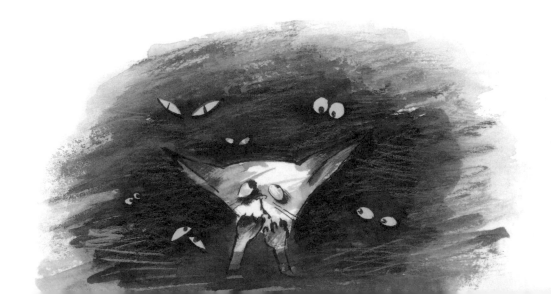

I could take a taxicab downtown, and find a job that would get me out of the house all day. I could work nights, too.

I'll be *Crispin the Working Cat!*

A gig as a cool cat modeling sunglasses might be fun.

Or I could get an easy job as a pet to a liver-loving lady.

Oh, who wants a job anyway? It's too much work.

I think I'll just hide out in the closet for the rest of my life. That'll teach them.

I'll be *Crispin the Invisible!*

Of course, it is a little lonely in a closet,
and there isn't much to do.

Do you think my family misses me?

Hey, what is all that racket?

I wonder what's going on out there.
Something awful must have happened!

WOW!

They're looking for *me*? They must really love me after all.

How could I have thought of deserting them?

Even if you have nine lives, you only have one family.

The truth is, I'm not very terrible or adventurous.

I'm just *Crispin the Family Cat!*